# This **Frog** book belongs to:

........................................

*This book is dedicated to all the animals on this earth,*
*whatever their colour or shade.*

This paperback edition first published in 2014 by Andersen Press Ltd.

20 Vauxhall Bridge Road, London SW1V 2SA.

First published in Great Britain in 1993 by Andersen Press Ltd.

Published in Australia by Random House Australia Pty.,

20 Alfred Street, Milsons Point, Sydney, NSW 2061.

Copyright © Max Velthuijs Foundation, 1993

The rights of Max Velthuijs to be identified as the author and illustrator

of this work have been asserted by him in accordance with the

Copyright, Designs and Patents Act, 1988.

All rights reserved.

Colour separated in Switzerland by Photolitho AG, Zürich.

Printed and bound in China by Foshan Zhao Rong printing Co., Ltd

10   9   8   7   6   5   4   3   2   1

British Library Cataloguing in Publication Data available.

ISBN  978 1 78344 143 3

# Frog
## and the Stranger

# Max Velthuijs

Andersen Press

One day, a stranger arrived and made a camp at the
edge of the woods. It was Pig who discovered him first.

"Have you seen him?" asked Pig excitedly when she met Duck and Frog.

"No. What's he like?" asked Duck.

"If you ask me, he looks like a filthy dirty rat," said Pig.

"What does he want here?"

"You have to be careful of rats," said Duck. "They're a thieving lot."

"How do you know?" asked Frog.

"Everyone knows," said Duck indignantly.

But Frog wasn't so sure. He wanted to see for himself.
That night, when darkness fell, he saw a red glow in
the distance.
Frog crept nearer.

At the edge of the wood he saw a couple of sticks with a rag draped over them, like a makeshift, untidy tent.

The stranger was cooking in a pot over a fire.
There was a wonderful smell and Frog thought
it all looked very cosy.

"I've seen him," Frog told the others, next day.
"And?" asked Pig.
"He looks like a nice fellow," said Frog.
"Be careful," said Pig. "Remember he's a dirty rat."
"I bet he'll eat all our food without ever doing a
day's work," said Duck. "Rats are cheeky and lazy."

But that wasn't true. Rat was always busy. He collected wood and skilfully made a table and bench.
He wasn't dirty either. He often bathed in the river, although he looked a little scruffy.

One day, Frog decided to visit Rat. Rat was sitting
resting on his new bench in the sun.
"Hello," said Frog. "I'm Frog."
"I know," said Rat. "I can see that. I'm not stupid.
I can read and write and I speak three languages –
English, French and German."
Frog was very impressed. Even Hare couldn't do that.

Just then Pig arrived.
"Where are you from?" she asked Rat angrily.
"From everywhere and nowhere," replied Rat calmly.
"Well, why don't you go back?" cried pig.
"You've no business here."
Rat remained calm.

"I have travelled all over the world," said Rat
unmoved. "It's peaceful here and there's a
wonderful view over to the river. I like it here."
"I bet you stole the wood," said Pig.
"I found it," said Rat in a dignified voice. "It belongs
to everyone."
"Dirty rat," muttered Pig.
"Yes, yes," said Rat bitterly. "Everything is always
my fault. Rat is always blamed for everything."

Frog, Pig and Duck went to visit Hare.

"That filthy rat must leave," said Pig.

"He's no right to be here. He steals our wood and is rude as well," cried Duck.

"Quiet, quiet," said Hare. "He may be different from us, but he's not doing anything wrong and the wood belongs to everyone."

From that day on, Frog went to visit Rat regularly. They sat side by side on the bench, enjoying the view, and Rat told Frog stories of his adventures round the world, for he had travelled widely and had had many exciting experiences.

Pig disapproved of Frog. "You shouldn't go round with that filthy rat," she said.

"Why not?" asked Frog.

"Because he's different from us," said Duck.

"Different," said Frog, "but we're all different."

"No," said Duck. "We belong together. Rat isn't from round here."

Then one day, Pig was careless while she was cooking. Flames leapt from the frying pan. Soon the fire spread and the flames were everywhere. The house was ablaze.

She ran outside terrified. "Fire! Fire!" she screamed. But Rat was already there. He hurried between the river and the house with buckets of water and fought the flames until the fire was out.

The roof of Pig's house was totally destroyed. All the animals stood round in shock. Now Pig was homeless. But she needn't have worried. The next day, Rat came round with a hammer and nails. As quick as a flash, the house was repaired!

Another time, Hare went to the river to fetch some water. Suddenly he slipped and fell into deep water. Hare couldn't swim.
"Help! Help!" he shouted loudly. It was Rat who heard the shouts at once and dived straight into the water. Quickly he rescued Hare and brought him to the safe, dry bank.

Everyone now agreed that Rat could stay. He was constantly happy and cheerful and was always there if someone needed help.

He often thought of fun things to do like having
a picnic by the river or a trip into the forest.

And during the evenings, he told them all exciting stories about dragons in China and other exciting things he had encountered in the world. It was a very happy time and Rat always had new tales to tell.

But one day, when Frog went to visit his friend
Rat he couldn't believe his eyes. The tent had
been taken down and Rat was standing there with his
rucksack.
"Are you leaving?" asked Frog in amazement.
"It's time to move on," said Rat. "I might go to
America. I've never been there." Frog was devastated.

With tears in their eyes, Frog, Duck, Hare and Pig
said goodbye to their friend Rat.
"Perhaps I'll come back one day," said Rat cheerfully.
"Then I'll build a bridge over the river."

Then he left – that filthy dirty, but nice, cheeky, helpful, clever Rat. They stared after him until he disappeared behind the hill.

"We'll miss him," said Hare with a sigh.

Yes, Rat left an empty space behind. But the bench was still there and the four friends often sat together on it and talked over their memories of their good friend Rat.

**Max Velthuijs's** twelve beautiful stories about **Frog** and his friends first started to appear twenty five years ago and are now available as paperbacks, e-books and apps.

9781783441440

9781783441532

9781783441501

9781783441426

9781783441471

9781783441457

9781783441525

97811783441433

9781783441518

9781783441495

9781783441488

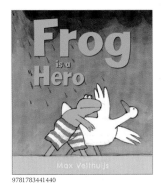
9781783441419

**Max Velthuijs** (Dutch for Field House) lived in the Netherlands, and received the prestigious Hans Christian Andersen Medal for Illustration. His charming stories capture childhood experiences while offering life lessons to children as young as three, and have been translated into more than forty languages.

'**Frog is an inspired creation – a masterpiece of graphic simplicity.**'
**GUARDIAN**

'**Miniature morality plays for our age.**' **IBBY**